Mrs Wrelton's Dinosaur

by

Ian MacDonald

Illustrated by Derry Dillon

First published
September 03 in Great Britain by

Educational Printing Services Limited
Albion Mill, Water Street, Great Harwood, Blackburn BB6 7QR
Telephone: (01254) 882080   Fax: (01254) 882010
e-mail: enquiries@eprint.co.uk   web site: www.eprint.co.uk

ISBN 1 904374-48-4

Contents

Mrs Wrelton's Dinosaur

Mrs Wrelton had a dinosaur. She kept it in the classroom on a table by the book corner. It was big and green and just a little bit scary. All along the length of its back, and all down its long tail, were triangle-spikes sticking up. Its mouth was fixed somewhere between a grin and a growl.

Ben said it was a Tyrannosaurus, Amy said it was a Brontosaurus, but Suhail, who knew everything about dinosaurs, said it was a Stegosaurus. But we all just called him Spike because of his tail. Everyone in the class loved Spike, but I loved him the best.

Spike was made of paper and glue. Mrs Wrelton told us that this was called papier-mâché. Her class had made it a very long time ago, she said.

"Perhaps long ago like when there WERE dinosaurs," whispered Suhail when she told us this. Suhail knows everything about dinosaurs.

Spike joined in everything we did in Mrs Wrelton's class. When we did numbers we counted on Spike's triangles. When it was painting we did pictures of Spike eating grass, or having a dinosaur fight. When we did plasticene models, me and Suhail and Amy made a whole family of little dinosaurs for Spike, and Mrs Wrelton put them on the shelf where Spike could see. I think he liked them a lot.

There were some things Spike did not do, like go to assembly, or when we went to climb on the apparatus in the hall. Then Spike stayed in the classroom. He did not like moving about so much.

When Mrs Wrelton called the register in the morning we sat on the carpet but Spike stayed on the table near the books. When Mrs Wrelton said, "Suhail," he said, "yes, Mrs Wrelton." When she said, "Amy," she said, "yes, Mrs Wrelton." When she said, "Sam," I said, "yes, Mrs Wrelton."

At the end she always said Spike's name. He never answered but I said it for him. I think that Mrs Wrelton knew it was me, but she never said anything. Then she marked Spike's name in the register. He had never had a day off for being ill, or buying shoes, or anything.

Spike always listened when it was story time. He liked it best when we had picture books about dinosaurs and I knew he was smiling then, even though he could not change his mouth. Sometimes, though, I thought that Spike must have been sad because there were no other dinosaurs to play with. But he had me. I was his best friend in the whole world.

One day, after we had been playing out on the bikes, and Spike was watching us out of the window, Mrs Shawcross came to see us. Mrs Shawcross is our Headteacher, and she is nice, though not as nice as Mrs Wrelton. We all had to sit on the carpet and listen.

Mrs Shawcross said she had something exciting to tell us.

"Do you remember that you are going to have a new classroom, children?" she began.

"Yes, Mrs Shawcross," we said.

It was true that we had watched the builders knocking down the old wooden buildings when we were in Class 1.

They had used big yellow diggers and our teachers had taken us out to see it. We all cheered to see the walls fall over so quickly. We were very little then. It was a very long time ago; though not as long ago as dinosaurs.

Then the builders had come and put bricks in piles everywhere, and when we looked each day there were new walls, and windows and a tiled roof. After a while nothing else seemed to happen and we stopped going to the fence to see. We went to play 'it', or kick a ball or play at dinosaurs instead.

"After the holiday you will be able to move into your new classroom," Mrs Shawcross continued. "It will be lovely.

There will be a new play-corner, new shelves for the books and a new sink for washing your hands."

Everyone looked at each other. It sounded very exciting.

"Before we finish for the holiday we will all have to have a big tidy-up. You must take home all your things at the end of the week. Mrs Wrelton will want you to help her clear up too."

Then she turned to Mrs Wrelton and said, "It will be a good opportunity to throw away some of the old things we don't need any more, old books, broken paint pots and *other things.*" When she said this, about the *other things*, she seemed to look at Spike, but then she just carried on talking.

"Tomorrow there will be a big yellow container on the playground. It's called a skip and it's for putting all the things in that you don't need anymore. Now mind you stay away from it, children, we don't want anyone falling in and getting hurt."

"No, Mrs Shawcross," said the others. I did not answer. I was too busy looking at Spike to see if he was alright. I don't think he was listening though.

Perhaps Mrs Shawcross did not mean Spike, she must have been looking at something else. Perhaps she meant the old computer that Mrs Wrelton did not like. It did not always work properly. It did not work very well when Ryan put his sandwich in the slot where the disks go. Perhaps that could go in the skip tomorrow.

That night I did not sleep very well. I worried about Spike and whether he would be safe. I dreamed about a big yellow monster that came and ate up Spike. When I woke up in the morning I was afraid to go to school in case anything had happened in the night.

At school everything was just the same except that the skip was on the playground.

We went to have a look. It was full of old chairs, desks, empty paint pots and rolls of old paper that had never been used. There were some of the classroom toys that had been broken or had bits missing: old jigsaw puzzles, torn books, a one armed teddy bear, two bikes with no wheels. I looked hard but I could not see Spike in the skip.

When the bell went I rushed in and Spike was there, sitting on the table. He was looking out of the window towards the skip. I thought that he looked a bit puzzled.

Mrs Wrelton called the register as usual and I said "yes" for Spike and me. While we did our numbers and painted and played in the sand Mrs Wrelton and Mrs Holland did some more tidying up. Lots more things went into boxes ready for the new classroom and other things went into black, plastic bags.

Suhail and me had to sharpen pencils and put them in baskets.

"If any are too small to use you can throw them away," said Mrs Wrelton, and she went off to do some more tidying.

"Will you sit next to me in the new class?" asked Suhail.

"Yes," I said, "as long as Amy can sit on

our table too. And as long as Spike sits somewhere where he can see us."

Suhail said this was a good idea and we talked about what it would be like in the new classroom.

Soon it was dinner time and we got our packed lunch boxes and went in to the dinner hall. Because the sun was shining we were allowed on the field. We ran in and out of the long grass and climbed on the log-cabin.

When we came back in the afternoon Spike was gone.

I looked out of the window and there he was, sitting on top of the desks and old chairs in the skip. He was leaning over slightly to one side and looking away to the playground so he could not see us. I wanted to go out and see him but all the children were already on the carpet listening to Mrs Wrelton.

"Have you seen Spike?" I whispered to Suhail.

"No, where has he gone?" said Suhail. He knew everything about dinosaurs, but he did not know what had happened to Spike.

"He's in the skip," I whispered, nodding my head in the direction of the window.

Suhail looked out of the window and saw the triangle spikes sticking up out of Spike's long green back.

"We've got to do something!"

"Sam, would you stop talking please! I'm trying to read a story," said Mrs Wrelton. She was a bit cross.

I kept quiet for the moment, but later, when Suhail was in the sandpit with Amy, I went over.

"We've got to do something about Spike," I said again.

"What can we do?" said Suhail, shrugging his shoulders.

"We're not allowed near the skip," said Amy, "Mrs Shawcross said so."

"Well, I'm going to do something even if you're not," I said crossly, and stomped off to the book corner on my own. I found some more pencils to sharpen. I sharpened them really hard so that some of them nearly disappeared.

Suddenly I had an idea!

I went over to the window where I could see Spike. Sitting up on top of all the old desks and chairs he looked somehow quite important, as if he was high up, keeping watch over the rest of the school. But I knew that the skip lorry would come soon and then he would be taken away and thrown onto a rubbish tip somewhere.

"It's going to be alright, Spike," I whispered, "I'm going to rescue you."

When it was home time I was the first to the door and I hardly dared to look at Spike in case anyone guessed what I was going to do.

At home I ate my burgers and beans in a hurry.

"Is something the matter?" Mum asked.

"Nothing. I'm fine." I said. "Mum?"

"Yes."

"Can I go to play at Suhail's?"

"Have you asked?"

"Yes," I lied, "it's O.K. He's said so, just until his dad gets home."

I often went round to Suhail's house. He had a whole collection of plastic dinosaurs and we were always playing with them. It was only three doors away and I was allowed to go there after dinner as long as Mum knew where I was.

"Alright then. Just for an hour mind," said Mum. "You've got the whole holidays to see Suhail, remember."

"Thanks," I said, and climbed down from my chair and hurried to the door before she changed her mind. I quickly ran upstairs looking for anything that might be useful. I could only see my torch.

Downstairs I collected my baseball cap, a jacket, and spotting Dad's golf set in the cupboard, I took the biggest club I could find . . . just in case there were monsters.

"Bye," called out Mum as I went out the door. I had already decided to try and persuade Suhail to come with me. I would call at his house and ask. If he did not want to come I would go anyway.

"I'm going to rescue Spike," I said to Suhail when he opened the door. "Are you going to help me or not?"

"I have to tidy my room," said Suhail, looking at his shoes. He was my friend and I could see that he wanted to come.

"Say you're going to my house," I whispered.

He hesitated a moment.

"Alright, wait here. I'll tell my Mum."

When he came back he was carrying his ray-gun that lights up when you press the trigger, and he was wearing his superhero mask too.

"Mind you come back in an hour," called out Mrs Bansel from the kitchen.

"Let's try Amy too," said Suhail when we had walked down the road just a little way. In another five minutes Amy had joined us. She was carrying a doll that said things when you pulled the chord. I was not sure what use this would be, but I did not say anything.

There were no roads to cross and in no time at all we were back at the school gate. It was just beginning to get dark. We stopped and listened.

"Get down low," I said in a loud whisper. "There might be people about."

It was now an hour and a half after school had closed but Mr Griffin the caretaker would be somewhere about. Some of the classrooms still had lights on and there were still three cars in the car park.

"When I say 'now', we'll go as far as the shed," I whispered.

Just then a big, yellow lorry turned in through the school gate, for a second its headlights lighting the whole car park. We waited until it had gone and then I shouted quietly, "NOW!"

Keeping our heads low we ran through the gate and stopped, panting, by the shed at the lower end of the playground. We listened but could not see anyone about.

"If we go round along the small playground there's less chance of anyone seeing us," I said.

I knew that there were bushes on this side of the school which we could hide in. Teachers would come across the other playground to get to the car park.

In a moment we were there. As we pushed further among the leaves it became harder to walk. It was like going through the jungle.

I put my torch on so that we could find the way. Once, Amy thought she saw a snake, but it was only a piece of old rope. Then, in front of us, there was a whole jumble of brambles.

"We'll have to go back," said Amy.

"No we won't," I said.

I took my Dad's best golf club and swung it at the tangle of prickly branches. Soon there was a pathway and we could go forward again. The golf club had a wooden bit on the end and it was now a bit scratched. I hoped Dad would not mind too much.

"Ssh!" said Suhail. "I can hear something."

Just then the light on the side of the school switched itself on. It made us jump. We peered onto the playground just in time to see the shadow of the biggest cat you ever saw. And it was coming this way.

The shadow stopped, its head right next to our hiding place. It sniffed the air.

"My hair needs brushing," said a squeaky voice.

We looked up and there, on the roof, standing in front of the light was the little ginger cat from next door.

"Can I wear my red dress?" said Amy's doll.

The cat did not like the voice and it turned and ran away into the darkness.

We had made our way past the first three classrooms now, past the office where Mrs Southall did the letters, and were nearly at the place where we hung our coats.

"Keep together," I whispered. "It's just around the corner now."

"But we've got to cross the playground to get there," said Suhail. "What if someone sees us?"

"We'll just have to take a chance."

"Can I go for a walk?" said Amy's doll.

Suhail and I both glared at Amy. She opened the doll's back, took out two batteries and put them in her pocket.

Pushing aside the branches of the last bush we stepped out onto the playground. There was no light here and dark shapes loomed out of the shadows. Suddenly we froze.

'THUMP!'

There was something right in front of us.

'BUMP!'

From out of the darkness came a large thing. It was green and had a black gaping mouth. It had no arms and legs but it was moving, bumping from side to side.

"It's an alien," shouted Suhail, and he lifted his ray gun and fired at the strange creature.

'Whoo! Whoo!' went the gun and the red light flashed.

It made no difference. The alien turned on its side and began to roll towards us.

"Aaah!"

"Help!"

"Mummy!"

Then it was quiet. I was the first to step out of the bushes. I turned my torch towards the place where the thing had gone. There, lying on its side, was the green litter bin. From out of the rectangular hole crept a small, grey squirrel clutching an apple core. It blinked at us in the torchlight, and then scampered away.

"Come on," said Amy, "let's hurry up and find Spike. I want to go home."

"The skip is just round the corner," I said. "Follow me."

One behind the other we crept to the corner of the building. There were no lights on inside but I could picture the classroom in my head as we went by. The sink would be cleaned and empty, there would be boxes of books ready for taking to the new room and the pictures would be taken down from the walls. Nothing would be the same anymore.

Then we were round the corner.

The skip had gone.

"Where is it?" hissed Suhail.

"Where's Spike?" asked Amy.

I did not say anything. I knew we were too late. I had let Spike down.

Back at my house Mrs Bansel and Mrs Johnson were both waiting.

"Where have you been?" asked my Mum.

I could see she was cross. They all were. We were grounded for the holiday. We were not allowed to see each other for a whole week. I did not mind that so much. It was missing Spike that I really minded.

I lay on the floor of my bedroom and drew pictures of Spike. I did so many that I filled a whole wall and the door of my wardrobe as well. Mum came and sat on my bed.

"What's the matter?" she said.

She listened as I tried to explain, but you could not explain to a grown up about having a dinosaur for a friend.

And then there was no more holiday left.

It was time to go back to school.

I picked up my bag and lunch box. Mum had bought me a new one with a Tyrannosaurus Rex on. I still did not want to go to school. Not without Spike.

Mrs Wrelton was there at the door of the new classroom.

"Come on in Sam," she said. "I've got something to show you."

Inside there were new pegs to hang our coats on, new pictures on the wall, a new sink that shone, and the books were all arranged on shelves in rainbow colours. Everything was bright and new; but I did not care.

"Look!" said Mrs Wrelton.

Taking my shoulder she led me around the next corner.

"This is your place," she said, "and your friend's already here."

And there, sitting at my table, was Spike.

"Spike," I shouted, and I ran and put my arms around him.

"I just couldn't throw him away after all," said Mrs Wrelton. "But we do need to find a good home for him. I don't think he will really like it here in the new classroom. Perhaps you know someone who could look after him properly."

"I could," I said.

"Could you?" said Mrs Wrelton.

"Good-night, Spike!" I said.

"Good-night, Sam!" said Spike.

Why not make your own papier mâché dinosaur?

Ask a grown up to help you.

Here are the things you need:
- some empty cereal boxes
- an old jug or bowl
- cellulose paste
- a paste brush
- tissue paper (or toilet roll)
- masking tape
- newspaper (lots)
- scissors

1. Make a rough shape for your dinosaur out of the cereal boxes. Join them together with masking tape. Other shapes, like triangle spikes, can be cut and taped onto the dinosaurs back.

2. Mix up the paste and water according to the packet instructions.

3. Now cover the dinosaur shape with several layers of tissue paper, pasting each layer with a brush. Allow to dry.

4. Now tear your newspaper into lots of little pieces and paste these over the whole model. Use the paper to mould the shapes that you need, the nostrils, eyes, claws etc. Add at least 5 or 6 more layers. Make sure there are no loose bits sticking up. Allow to dry.

5. Paint your dinosaur green (although no-one really knows what colour real dinosaurs were!)

6. Make friends with your dinosaur!

Spike's Tail

It was dark. The curtains moved gently at the window making shadows on the carpet. I blinked my eyes, trying to see the shapes in the room. "It must be the middle of the night," I thought.

Somewhere I could hear the sound of scratching. Was there someone at the window? Was there a monster at the door? I pulled the duvet tightly over my ears. It was a good thing that there was a dinosaur in my bed!

"Sam, are you up yet?"

No answer.

'CREAK'!

Slowly the door opened. The dark shape of a head peered round into the gloom of my bedroom. It was only Monster Mum! (She's not really a monster. She's just my mum . . . and she's quite nice most days.)

"Good morning, Sam," said Monster Mum.

"Good morning, Mum," I said, poking my head out from under the duvet.

"Good morning, Spike," said Mum.

"Good Morning, Monster Mum," said Spike.

He poked his green head out too. He was feeling a bit cheeky. Mum pretended to look cross but she was smiling underneath. Spike had not really said that. I often said his words for him because he could not move his mouth. Besides, he had not fully woken up yet.

Spike was my dinosaur. He was made out of paper and glue. He was very handsome. He had green triangle spikes all sticking up and down his back, from the top of his head to the tip of his long tail. His mouth was fixed somewhere between a grin and a growl.

Spike used to live in Mrs Wrelton's class at school, but the classroom had just got too busy for a dinosaur. Mrs Wrelton said Spike could come and live at my house. We had room because we haven't got a sand pit or a reading corner in any of the rooms where we live.

Everyone in the class loved Spike; but I loved him the best.

Mum pulled back the curtains. It was morning after all.

"Come on, Sam. We're off to the dinosaur museum today, remember?"

"Great!" I said.

"Yippee!" said Spike.

It was true. It was the holidays and Mum said she would take us to the museum. She had said I could ask a friend. It was hard to choose. Amy was one of my best friends. She could kick a ball all the way to the other end of the playground. She could make her eyes look like an alien. But, in the end, it had to be Suhail because he knew just about everything about dinosaurs.

"Come on Sam, Suhail's here," called out Mum.

Breakfast was over and I was just finding my coat and baseball cap from my room. I hurried downstairs to find Mum and Suhail waiting.

"I've just got to get Spike," I said.

Mum looked at me. "I'm afraid Spike can't come," she said.

"But we're going to see dinosaurs. How can we leave Spike behind?" I said, and I could feel the tears coming to my eyes.

"He's too big to take on the train."

"But I could carry him. I wouldn't mind."

"I'm sorry love, but it will be far too busy in London for a big, green dinosaur."

"But he could come instead of Suhail," I said.

As soon as the words came out I knew it had been a bad thing to say. Then Suhail started to cry too.

Mum did that thing where she put her eyes toward the ceiling and sighed. "It's no good, Sam. We'll be late. Come on both of you."

We went out of the house and down the road.

"Please, Mum!" I said.

We went across the main road and past the newspaper shop.

"Please! He won't be any trouble."

We went through the alley that leads to the station.

"Please, I'll carry him everywhere, and I won't complain, and Spike will be really good!"

Soon we were standing in the queue to buy our ticket at the train station. First there was Mum.

Then there was Suhail.

Then there was me.

And then there was Spike.

He was wearing my baseball cap in case he got cold on the way.

"Let me see," said the man when we got to the counter. "There's your tickets, one adult and two boys." The man peered out through the glass window. He took off his cap and scratched his head. "I'm not so sure about your dragon though."

"He's not a dragon; he's a dinosaur," I said.

"He's a Stegosaurus," said Suhail.

"He's called Spike," I added.

"Oh, I see," said the ticket man and he looked at Spike. Then he opened a big book and began turning the pages.

"Let's see . . . cats . . . dogs . . . parrots." He shook his head. "I can't see anything here about green dinosaurs!"

He looked at me and winked. "I suppose we'll just have to let him go free then, won't we?"

As we went out onto the platform there was a red ticket on the floor. It did not seem to belong to anyone. Spike had no ticket so I picked it up. Someone had made a hole in it but you could still see the words. I stuck it in the front of Spike's baseball cap. He looked pleased.

On the train I sat Spike next to the window so he could see out. Mum and Suhail sat opposite on the other seat. From out of the window we saw fields and trees, cows and sheep, and a farmer on his tractor. But soon we would see dinosaurs.

"Suhail," I whispered, "I'm sorry about what I said, about taking Spike instead of you."

"That's O.K.," he said. "I would have said the same."

Suhail was my best friend after Spike and he knew everything about dinosaurs. He knew you couldn't leave a dinosaur behind when you were going to a dinosaur museum.

An old lady got in when we stopped at a station. She was struggling with a big case and she wore a purple hat with feathers on it. The hat was half-hanging off her head. There were not many seats because the train was busy. She stopped next to where I was sitting. When she saw Spike she blinked and her hat fell onto the floor.

Mum picked it up for her, dusted off the feathers, and smiled. She moved our bags and offered the lady the seat next to me. But the woman shook her head and hurried on to the next carriage. I don't think she wanted to sit by a green dinosaur with a red ticket in his baseball cap.

After a while Mum said that we had to change at the next station. She said we were going on the underground. There were lights on the ceiling, and metal stairs that went up and down all by themselves, and pictures on the walls, but not like the ones at school.

"This is called an escalator," said Mum, as we were going down.

"Ess-key-later," said Spike. He had not

51

been on one before. There were not any
escalators in dinosaur times. If you wanted
to go up a mountain you just had to walk.

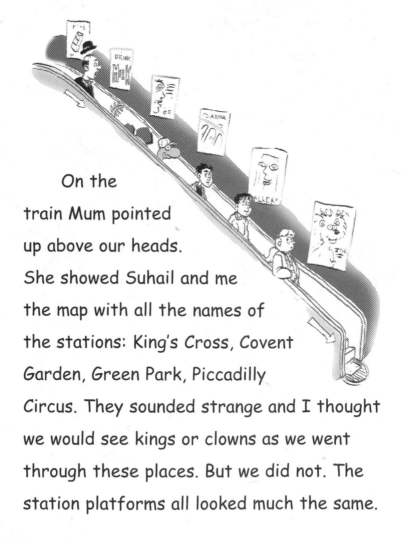

On the
train Mum pointed
up above our heads.
She showed Suhail and me
the map with all the names of
the stations: King's Cross, Covent
Garden, Green Park, Piccadilly
Circus. They sounded strange and I thought
we would see kings or clowns as we went
through these places. But we did not. The
station platforms all looked much the same.

"Come on," said Mum, "we're here. Time to get off."

Through the window I could see the name of the station.

"This is Kensington. It's where the dinosaur museum is," said Mum.

I picked up Spike and we stood at the sliding doors.

'PSSHH' went the sliding doors and we stepped out onto the platform.

I looked down and my shoelace had come undone. I put Spike down next to me.

'PSSHH . . . BIFF . . . CRUMP'.

Spike jumped. He had never jumped before. When I looked round at Spike his tail was gone.

"Look," said Suhail, pointing, "the train has eaten Spike's tail!"

Spike was standing in Kensington . . . but his tail was going to Piccadilly Circus.

"Mum! Mum! The doors have bitten off Spike's tail!" I shouted, but it was too late. The train had already left the station. I began to cry.

Suhail knew everything about dinosaurs, but he did not know Spike was going to have his tail bitten off by a train.

"Never mind," said Mum, taking a tissue from her bag. "Spike will be alright. When we get to the museum it will take his mind off it."

But I could not forget about Spike's tail. All the way to the museum I kept looking at the place where his tail should have been.

I put Spike under my arm and hoped that people would not notice. Some people looked, but most people seemed to be in too much of a hurry to notice a green dinosaur with a red ticket in his baseball cap . . . and no tail.

There was another moving staircase and we had to get on. I held onto Spike's hand. We began to go up. It was very busy. Some people were in a hurry and they were running up the escalator. And then a man brushed against me and I let go of Spike. He went bumping down, all the way to the bottom.

'BUMP. Bump. Crump'.

"Mum! Mum! Spike's gone down the up-stairs!"

And then we were at the top and I saw the other stairs going down. I did not wait to ask.

Before Mum could grab me I dashed round and jumped on. I held on to the black rail and I could hear Mum shouting, "Sam, come back!" But it was too late to turn round.

I looked down but I could not see Spike anywhere. There were lots of people going by on the up-stairs as I was going the other way; people in smart jackets, people in colourful scarves, mums with children, and men carrying newspapers. In the middle of them all was a green dinosaur. Spike had not waited for me. He had found a nice lady to carry him back up. Clever Spike! Mum was waiting for me at the top with Suhail and Spike. She was not pleased.

"Let's get to this museum before anything else happens," she said.

When we got to the dinosaur museum it was enormous. The roof seemed to nearly touch the sky. The first room was full of people looking at booklets and buying tickets, grown ups with children and grown ups on their own, and there were two women in uniforms behind a desk. On every side were big pillars with pictures on them, pictures of strange creatures, faces, fruit and plants.

Mum bought tickets to go in. Spike did not need one. Dinosaurs were allowed in a dinosaur museum without a ticket.

"Look at all these beautiful things," said Mum, as we went into the next hall which was all about plants and flowers.

But I did not want to look. I just could not stop thinking about Spike.

"Look!" said Suhail. "A whole room full of wild animals."

Suhail ran in and pressed his nose up against the glass.

"Wow!"

There were lions, and tigers, and elephants, and bears, and all kinds of creatures. They all looked real, but they could not have been because they did not move or make a noise. All of them had tails.

"Come on," said Mum, "we've come all this way to see the museum and you're not even looking. We will just have to forget about Spike for the time being and try and enjoy ourselves."

I did not say anything. I could see Spike was cross. But not as cross as Mum.

We went into the room where the sea animals were. There was the whole skeleton of a whale. You could go and stand inside it. I did not bother.

"Look, a whale!" said Suhail. "It's nearly as big as a Brontosaurus. I'm standing in its tummy! It's eaten me! I'm all eaten up!"

I did not want to take Spike inside a whale. He had been nearly eaten once today already. I was not taking any chances.

Mum looked at me. "Perhaps it's time for us to have something to eat," she said. "We could go and have a burger in the restaurant, and then we can go and see the dinosaurs."

In the restaurant Mum bought burgers and chips. They came in a box with pictures of dinosaurs on it.

"Look," said Suhail, "that's a Tyrannosaurus fighting a Stegosaurus."

I did not look but I knew that the dinosaurs on the box all had tails. Big ones with triangle spikes sticking up. Suhail put some tomato ketchup on his chip and put it on the Stegosaurus picture.

"Look the Tyrannosaurus is winning," said Suhail.

"Don't play with your food, Suhail," said Mum. "Sam, you've not eaten your burger. Aren't you hungry?"

I just looked at my cold chips.

"Well, there won't be anything else until we get home," said Mum, "and that's going to be a long time."

Then it was time to go and see the dinosaurs.

"Wow!" said Suhail when we got into the hall.

There were dinosaurs everywhere.

There were pictures and diagrams showing where dinosaurs lived. There were televisions telling you what dinosaurs had for dinner. There were glass cases with models showing dinosaurs being born and growing up, and there were real dinosaurs just standing there as big as anything.

A family of Brontosaurs were munching on some leaves. Some smaller dinosaurs were guarding their eggs. A Stegosaurus, just like Spike, was putting its head up to see what was going on.

At the next place there was a big Tyrannosaurus Rex. It was standing over a smaller dinosaur as if it was about to attack.

The Tyrannosaurus could move its head and legs, and make a loud noise.

Suddenly, it turned its head and seemed to look straight at Spike and me.

'ROAR' went the big Tyrannosaurus.

'Roar' went Spike. I could tell Spike just did not feel like roaring properly when not all of him was there.

Suhail stood at the bars and jumped up and down when the Tyrannosaurus growled.

"Come on, Suhail," said Mum. "There's lots more to see. What's this one called?"

As we walked away from the place where the Tyrannosaurus was making a noise there was a quieter place away from the rest of the hall. There were not so many people about here. Mum found a bench and sat down.

Nearby, behind a rail, a man was working. It looked like he was making a jigsaw out of sticks. I dragged my feet and pulled Spike along behind me. Suhail pushed by to take a better look.

"It's a dinosaur skeleton," shouted Suhail. "Come and see, Sam."

Mum got up and leaned over the rail
see what the man was doing. Suhail put his
head through the railings. I hung back. A
skeleton was not a real dinosaur, not like the
other ones that moved and growled.

The man looked up. Perched on the end
of his nose was a pair of round glasses. His
hands were covered in a white powder.

"Hello," he said. "What's your name?"

When I looked to see who the man was
talking to, it was not Suhail. He was not
looking at Mum. He was not even looking at
me. He was talking to Spike.

"His name's Spike," I said, "and he's my
dinosaur."

I stepped forward so that the man could see him. But I turned Spike around so that the man could not see the place where his tail was gone.

"What kind of dinosaur is he?" asked the man.

"He's a Stegosaurus," said Suhail.

"Of course!" said the man. "He's a very fine Stegosaurus, too."

"What are you doing?" I asked the man.

"Well," said the man, standing up. "This is the skeleton of a Pterodactyl. It was a flying dinosaur, something like a giant bird. This creature died millions of years ago, and someone found its skeleton in a piece of rock out in Mexico."

"Why is it here then?" I said.

"It looks like a jigsaw puzzle," said Suhail.

"It is a bit like that," laughed the man. "It's my job to put it all together, the bits that are here, and the bits that aren't."

"You mean that there are bits missing?" I asked.

"That's right," the man went on. "When something is this old you are lucky if you find a whole skeleton. Usually some of it has been lost and you have to make up the part that is longer there. It's a bit like having a jigsaw when someone's lost some of the bits."

"What's that stuff there?" said Suhail, pointing to a pot of white mixture. It looked something like the mixture I had seen Mum use to make cakes at home.

"That's what I use for making the missing bones."

"You're a dinosaur repair man," I said.

On the train going home we sat near the lady with the big feather hat. I wondered what kind of bird the feather came from. Perhaps she had bought the hat at the time when there were dinosaurs. Perhaps it was a Pterodactyl feather.

The old lady kept looking at Spike. She had seen him once already that day. She could tell there was something different about him.

It was not his green, scaly skin.

It was not his triangle spikes sticking up along his back.

It was not even the red ticket that was tucked into the front of his baseball cap.

It was . . . . .

his shiny, new, white tail.

Also available

by

Ian MacDonald

Assembly Lines

ISBN 1 904374 49 2

Published by
Educational Printing Services Limited
September 2003